Good Dog School

Adapted by **Tina Gallo**
based on the screenplay **"Good Dog School"**
written by **Stephanie D'Abruzzo**

Ready-to-Read

Simon Spotlight
New York London Toronto Sydney New Delhi

SIMON SPOTLIGHT
An imprint of Simon & Schuster Children's Publishing Division
1230 Avenue of the Americas, New York, New York 10020
This Simon Spotlight edition June 2022

Donkey Hodie is produced by Fred Rogers Productions and Spiffy Pictures.

For information about special discounts for bulk purchases, please contact
Simon & Schuster Special Sales at 1-866-506-1949
or business@simonandschuster.com.
Manufactured in the United States of America 0522 LAK
10 9 8 7 6 5 4 3 2 1
ISBN 9781665911702 (hc)
ISBN 9781665911696 (pbk)
ISBN 9781665911719 (ebook)

Bob Dog hopes to graduate (say: GRAH-joo-ate) from Good Dog School today!

“I have to tap-dance, sit and stay, and bake muffins to graduate,”

Bob Dog said to his friends,

Donkey Hodie and

Purple Panda.

“But I am nervous!
What if I do not remember
how to do everything?”
Bob Dog asked.

"I, Donkey Hodie,
will help you graduate!"
Donkey said.
"Me too!" said Panda.

“How can we help?
Think, Donkey Hodie,
think!” Donkey said.
“I know!”

"The first thing you need to do is tap-dance. These bongo drums remind me of something," Donkey said.

"I remember!" Bob Dog said.
"You played the bongos,
and I started tapping my feet.
I called it 'paw-drumming'!"

"You were really good at it!" said Donkey.

"If I feel nervous at graduation,
I will remember how good
I was at paw-drumming!"
Bob Dog said.

“But what if I cannot
do my ‘sit and stay’?”
Bob Dog asked.

Now Panda had an idea!

"Remember when I drew this picture of you?" Panda asked.

"I told you to hold
that pose, and
you stayed still!"

“Yes, I did!” Bob Dog nodded. “When I have to sit and stay at graduation,

I will remember how good I was at staying still for that picture!”

"Now I just need a way to remember how to bake muffins," Bob Dog said.

"Do you remember when you made us a big, tasty cake?" Donkey asked.

“Yes!” Bob Dog said.
“So when I have to bake
muffins at graduation,

I will remember how I made that big, tasty cake!"

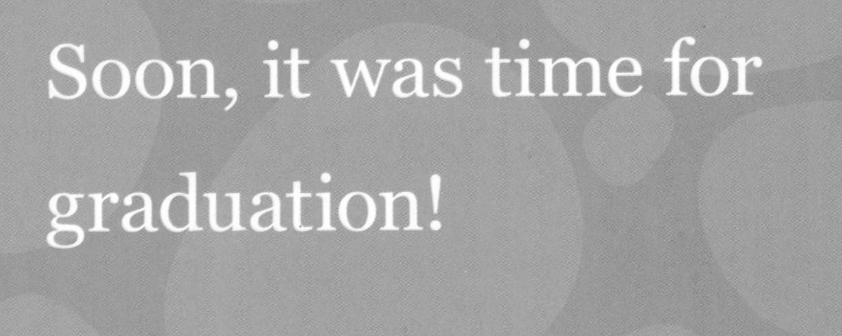

Soon, it was time for graduation!

"You can do it!"
Donkey and Panda
cheered.

First Bob Dog had to tap-dance. He thought of how good he was at paw-drumming, and he did it!

Next Bob Dog had to sit and stay. He remembered how he sat still when Panda drew his picture, and that helped him stay still now.

Lastly, he had to bake muffins. He remembered his big, tasty cake, and that helped him bake the muffins now!

He did it! Bob Dog
graduated from
Good Dog School!

"Bow wow, I did it!
Thank you for helping me,"
Bob Dog said to
Donkey and Panda.

"You were hee-hawesome!" Donkey cheered.

"Hey-o!" Panda added.

Everyone celebrated
with muffins.
Bob Dog was indeed
a very good dog!